Cold Whispers II

NIGHTMARE in the HIDDEN MORGUE

by Dee Phillips

illustrated by Tom Connell

BEARPORT
PUBLISHING

New York, New York

Credits
Cover, © Kankaitom/Shutterstock and © coka/Shutterstock.

Publisher: Kenn Goin
Senior Editor: Joyce Tavolacci
Creative Director: Spencer Brinker

Library of Congress Cataloging-in-Publication Data in process at time of publication (201
Library of Congress Control Number: 2016019101
ISBN-13: 978-1-944102-34-0 (library binding)

For more information, write to Bearport Publishing Company, Inc.,
45 West 21st Street, Suite 3B, New York, New York 10010.
Printed in the United States of America.

10 9 8 7 6 5 4 3 2 1

Contents

CHAPTER 1

The New House

After stepping out of their car, Zach's family looked at their new house.

"It's got towers like a castle!" yelled Zach.

"I think it's creepy," said Sophie.

"Look at all the weeds," said Dad, with a big sigh.

"It needs a lot of work, but we'll fix it up in no time," Mom said cheerily.

She was right. This wasn't the first time Zach and Sophie's parents had bought a **dilapidated** old house to **renovate**.

The huge house looked as if no one had taken care of it for decades. A jungle of tall grass **obscured** the first floor. In many places, the paint was faded and peeling. Some of the windows were closed up as if the building were hiding a secret.

"Come on," said Dad. "Let's check out our new house."

Zach and his family walked up to the front porch. Dad unlocked the front door with an ancient-looking skeleton key. The door opened with a long, loud creak.

As the family walked into the hallway, their footsteps echoed throughout the house.

"Mom and Dad, is it okay if I explore? Can I have a bedroom in one of the towers?" asked Zach excitedly as he ran up a wide staircase.

"Yes," Mom said as she, Sophie, and Dad walked to the kitchen. "Just be careful. No one has lived in this house for ages, and the previous owners left a lot of old stuff behind."

At the top of the stairs, Zach found a long, gloomy hallway. Down the hall, he could see a wooden door set into the curved wall of the **turret**. Zach ran to the door and shoved it open.

Inside the room, heavy curtains and shutters blocked out the late afternoon sun. Even in the dim light, Zach could see the room's rounded walls. He walked to the window and opened the long curtains. A cloud of thick dust rose up like smoke from the old fabric. Then dozens of **mummified** bugs fell onto his head. Startled, Zack stepped backward and batted the bugs out of his hair. Then he suddenly felt something soft brush against his cheek.

Hanging from the curtains, with one of its tiny wings caught in the fabric, was a dead bird. All that remained of the little creature was a fragile skeleton and some wing feathers. Zach shook the curtains. The bird fell to the floor, finally free.

Zach bent down and gently picked up the small animal. Then he looked at an old metal bed and a large antique dresser in the room. Sitting on top of the dresser was a black top hat. It was so thick with dust that it looked gray.

"Zach, time for dinner!" yelled his mom from the kitchen.

Zach walked to the dresser and carefully laid the skeleton near the top hat. Then he hurried downstairs.

After dinner, Zach grabbed his sleeping bag and headed back upstairs to spend his first night in his new bedroom.

Dad came, too, and together they tidied up the room, sweeping up all the dust and the dead bugs.

"Get some rest, kiddo," said Dad, as Zach finally climbed into his sleeping bag. "Good night. And don't let the dead bugs bite!" Dad said with a smile.

After a long and exciting day, Zach fell fast asleep.

Zach stirred as he felt a burst of cold air around him. He opened his eyes, but could see nothing but blackness. Shivering, he tried to figure out where he was and why the air around him was so cold. It felt as if he were sleeping in a refrigerator.

Confusion and fear began to spread from his stomach into his chest. Zach tried to take a deep breath, but he couldn't get enough air. It was as if he were . . . **suffocating!**

A terrible feeling of panic flooded his body. He couldn't breathe . . . and he was trapped in icy blackness.

A strangled cry for help burst from Zach's mouth as he woke up with a jolt.

Panting for breath, Zack realized he was inside his sleeping bag in his new bedroom. Moonlight filtered in through the window. He could see the room's curved walls, and the black top hat and the bird's skeleton on the dresser.

Zack switched on his flashlight for comfort, and then wrapped himself up tight in his sleeping bag. Finally, he closed his eyes and tried hard not to think about the terrifying dream.

CHAPTER 2

Blood in the Basement

The next morning at breakfast, with the nightmare a fuzzy memory, Zach turned to his younger sister, Sophie. "I found a dead bird and an old top hat yesterday," he said, hoping to get a reaction out of her.

"A dead bird? That's gross!" squealed Sophie.

Then Zach turned to his parents and said, "I saw a small door under the stairs. Does it lead to the basement? Can I check it out?"

"I want to see the basement, too," said Sophie.

"Yes, kids. Just take a flashlight. The light switch in the basement doesn't work," said Dad. "If you need us, Mom and I will be on the front porch waiting for the moving truck."

Zach and Sophie finished breakfast, grabbed a flashlight, and headed for the basement door. They tugged on the door and it opened stiffly. Zach turned on his flashlight and shined it down the narrow wooden steps.

A terrible **stench** filled Zach's nostrils. The smell reminded him of the time he found a **decomposing** fox on the street near his school.

At the bottom of the stairs, Zach waved the flashlight around. The basement was crammed with furniture and boxes. He chose a pathway through the clutter and crept forward.

"Aaarrrgghh!" screamed Zach. His head was suddenly wrapped in a giant sticky spiderweb.

He handed the flashlight to Sophie and plucked the web off his face.

"Look!" she said, pointing the flashlight at a large wooden **armoire** at the very back of the basement.

They squeezed past several stacks of chairs with red velvet seats to reach the armoire.

Zach pulled open one of the armoire's doors. To his disappointment, it was empty.

As Zach pushed the door shut, his foot slid in something thick and slimy. "Yuck," he said taking the flashlight from Sophie and shining it on the floor.

A pool of dark-colored liquid oozed from underneath the armoire.

Zach touched the pool and then held his hand under the light.

"It's blood!" Sophie screamed.

"Come on!" shouted Zach, as he quickly wiped his hand on his pants. "We have to get Mom and Dad."

They scrambled back through the basement and up the stairs.

"Mom! Dad!" yelled Zach and Sophie.

Mom was helping Dad carry a heavy box from the moving truck.

"There's blood on the floor in the basement," cried Zach, his voice trembling.

"There's . . . what?" said Dad, alarmed. "Blood, are you sure?" Zach's parents set down the box, and they all headed to the basement. As they approached the armoire, Zach aimed the flashlight on the floor.

"There's nothing there, Zach," said Dad, as he looked around and checked inside the armoire.

To Zach's amazement, the pool of blood had disappeared. He looked down. There was no blood on his pants or shoes either!

Mom sighed and began to head back toward the stairs. "Come on, guys," she said. "I think your imaginations are running away with you in this old house."

As he followed his parents and Sophie back up the stairs, Zach was sure it wasn't his imagination. The feel of the slippery blood beneath his foot was still **vivid** in his memory. And all around him, the horrible smell of rotting flesh **lingered**.

Later that afternoon, Zach carried a box of his things from the moving truck to his bedroom. Now, wherever he went in the house, he could smell the terrible stench from the basement.

Mom was in his bedroom taking down the old dusty curtains.

"Mom?" said Zach. "Do you smell something weird?"

Mom sniffed the air and looked around the room. Her gaze fell on the dead bird on the dresser.

"Zach," she said. "You have a dead bird in your bedroom. It's hardly surprising you smell something weird."

Zach knew the smell wasn't coming from the long-dead bird, but he decided to take the animal outside and bury it. He found a rusty spade on the back porch and dug a hole in the yard.

As he knelt on the ground, something caught his eye in the window of his bedroom. At first, he thought it was his mother. But then Zach realized the figure was hunched over like an old man . . . and was wearing a top hat.

With a chill running down his spine, Zach rushed back into the house, up the stairs, and into his room.

Mom stood up from unpacking a box. "What is it, Zach?" she said.

Zach looked around the room in disbelief. There was no hunched figure, and the top hat was exactly where he had left it on the dresser.

Zach opened his eyes. He turned his head to the left and right, expecting to see his bedroom, but there was nothing but blackness. Once again, the air was icy cold.

Zach reached into the darkness for a blanket and his fingers struck icy metal. He tried to sit up, but his head banged into hard metal just a few inches above his face.

Zach began to shake. He reached out his hands, desperately feeling all around him. He was trapped inside an ice-cold metal box . . . a box shaped like a coffin!

He gasped for breath. "Mom! Dad!" he screamed, but no sound came out of his mouth.

Filled with terror, he pushed and kicked the cold metal. . . .

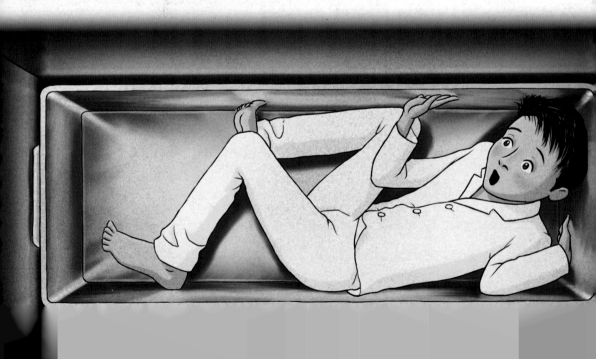

With a crash, Zach fell out of bed onto the bare floorboards. He'd had another horrible nightmare.

Zach's heart was beating fast as he **clambered** back into bed. As he lay shaking in his bedroom, he noticed the terrible smell still hanging in the air.

Something strange and horrible was going on inside the old house. And Zach had to find out what it was.

CHAPTER 3

The Secret Room

The next morning, while his parents were busy unpacking, Zach opened the door to the basement and began to climb down the stairs.

"Wait for me, Zach," called Sophie from the top of the stairs.

Zach was relieved to have his sister's company.

They walked to the armoire. Zach directed the flashlight's beam onto the floor. He and Sophie gasped. Just as on the previous day, a puddle of dark red blood seeped from under it.

"Where's the blood coming from?" asked Zach.

Together, he and Sophie pushed hard on one side of the armoire. With an ear-piercing shriek, it slid sideways.

Behind the armoire was a large metal door with a lever-like handle.

"It's a secret room," whispered Sophie, nervously.

Zach reached for the handle and pushed it down. The heavy door swung open.

A strange buzzing noise filled the air. Then *ping, ping.* Two bulbs hanging from the room's ceiling flickered on.

Zach and Sophie walked into the large, cold room, which was covered with white tiles. One wall was completely filled with shelves and cabinets. In the center of the room was a long table with a large drain beneath it.

Zach and Sophie slowly crossed the room to look at the shelves. They saw a tray that included **scalpels** and a small saw.

"What's this, Zach?" asked Sophie, holding up a jar.

Zach peered into the **murky**, yellow liquid. Floating in the jar was a lumpy, jelly-like object.

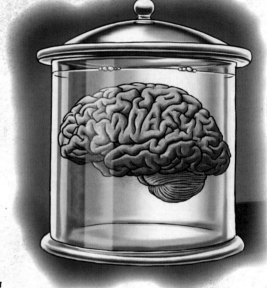

"Ugh!" said Zach, backing away from the jar. "It's someone's brain. Put it down!"

Sophie screamed, dropping the jar onto the floor. As the jar shattered, a strong chemical smell floated up from the liquid. The gray, mushy brain lay on the hard floor among the shards of glass.

"I think I'm going to be sick," Sophie cried, covering her mouth.

Zach watched as the liquid from the jar trickled down the room's gently sloping floor and disappeared down the drain.

Zach tore his eyes away from the mess and continued looking around. That's when he noticed that one entire wall was covered with rows of large metal drawers.

Zach crossed the room and cautiously reached for the handle of one of the drawers. It had a discolored label on the outside. Zach pulled on the handle. A whoosh of icy air escaped as the drawer slid open revealing a pair of gray, shriveled feet poking from under a white sheet. The drawer contained a **corpse!**

Zach quickly closed the drawer so Sophie couldn't see what was inside. It was then he realized the secret room beneath their house was a **morgue!** Did the other drawers also hold dead bodies?

Almost too afraid to look, he pulled open a second drawer and peered inside. To his relief, it was empty.

"Zach, look out!" Sophie's voice suddenly broke the silence.

He turned quickly to see blood bubbling up from the drain in the center of the room. The pool of dark, red blood flowed across the floor toward his feet.

"Sophie, get out of here," Zach shouted.

She hesitated for a second, and then fled out of the door and into the basement.

Zach tried to back away from the blood, but his feet slid in the slippery liquid and flew out from underneath him. He clawed hopelessly at the air to try to steady himself but fell backward, hitting his head on the floor. Then everything in the room started spinning.

As his head **reeled** from the fall, Zach felt his body being lifted off the floor. He squinted his eyes and saw that he was being carried by the hunched old man—the same ghostly creature he'd seen standing at his bedroom window. Zach was so afraid he couldn't move. Then the man placed Zach into one of the morgue drawers as if he were a corpse!

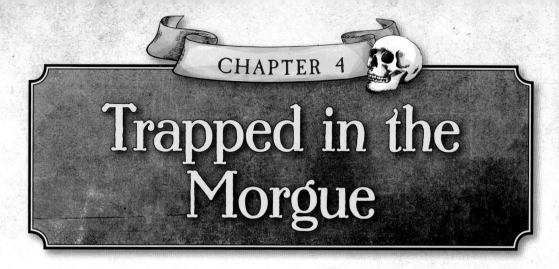

CHAPTER 4

Trapped in the Morgue

The old man pushed the drawer into the wall. *Bang!* Zach was now fully awake. He realized he was trapped inside a freezing cold metal box—just like in his nightmare!

Zach tried hard to think. He'd seen Sophie run from the morgue. She would tell Mom and Dad what they'd found in the basement. Help would arrive soon . . . wouldn't it?

As he lay in the drawer trembling with fear, Zach noticed that it was open just enough for him to see into the room.

Zach saw the hunched old man walking toward a cabinet. Instead of a black coat and top hat, he wore a long white coat covered with bloodstains.

Zach watched as the **mortician** carefully collected a rubber tube, scalpels, and a small saw and placed them on the table. Next, he lifted a large jar of pink liquid with a label that read **embalming** fluid. Zach realized the mortician was about to prepare a dead body for burial!

Once everything was in place on the table, the old mortician turned and shuffled toward the wall of drawers. He then reached for the one Zach was in. Zach let out a bloodcurdling scream.

"Zach! Zach! Shush. It's okay, honey." It was his Mom's comforting voice. Sophie, looking worried, stood nearby.

Confused and terrified, Zach suddenly found himself looking into his family's anxious faces as the drawer he was inside was pulled open.

"Hiding in that drawer was not a smart thing to do," said Dad.

Confused, Zach clambered from the drawer, his legs like jelly. He pushed past his mom and dad and Sophie to look at the table in the center of the room. There was no blood. And there was no sign of the ghostly mortician.

Zach rushed back to the drawers and started pulling them open. Every drawer was empty. "There was a . . . a body. And . . . an . . . an old man in a white coat, and . . ." Zach's voice faded away as he realized how crazy it all sounded.

"What is this place, anyway?" said Mom, staring in horror all around her.

"It looks like a morgue," said Dad, as he peered into a glass jar that held some kind of body part. "This old house must have been used as a funeral home."

27

The family headed upstairs to the kitchen. Dad wrapped his arm around Zach. Everyone sat down at the table, and Mom made hot chocolate.

As Sophie sipped from her steaming mug, she said, "I hate this house."

"Don't worry," said Mom giving Sophie a reassuring hug. "The **contractors** are coming tomorrow to work on the house. I'll make sure the first thing they'll do is rip out that awful room in the basement."

The next morning, Zach and Sophie sat on the front porch and watched the contractors throw the contents of the morgue into a big yellow Dumpster.

Zach suddenly remembered that he had something he needed to throw away, too. He quickly ran to his room and came back downstairs, holding the top hat. He tossed it onto the heap.

As he stood looking at the crumpled morgue drawers and other gruesome equipment piled in the Dumpster, he thought back to the terrifying time he'd spent trapped in the morgue.

Once the Dumpster was full, Zach and Sophie watched as it was hauled away. They turned to look up at the old house and gave a big sigh of relief.

Zach then headed upstairs to his room and jumped onto his bed, exhausted from the horrifying ordeal. Just as he was about to close his eyes, Zach noticed something on his dresser. An overwhelming sense of panic flooded his body. There, sitting exactly where it had been before he tossed it out, was the dusty black top hat.

WHAT DO YOU THINK?

Nightmare in the Hidden Morgue

1. What two unusual items does Zach find in his new bedroom?

2. What happens to Zach during his first night in the new house?

3. Why does Zach believe something strange is going on in the house? Use examples from the story to explain.

4. What is Zach feeling and experiencing in this scene?

5. Zach's new house was once a funeral home. What clues to the house's history appear in the story?

GLOSSARY

armoire (ARHM-wahr) a tall piece of furniture with doors

clambered (KLAM-burd) climbed with difficulty

contractors (KON-trak-turz) people who perform work for a fee

corpse (KORPS) a dead body

decomposing (dee-kuhm-POHZ-ing) rotting

dilapidated (dih-LAP-i-day-tid) fallen into ruin

embalming (im-BAHLM-ing) something used to treat a dead body to prevent decay

lingered (LING-gurd) stayed in one place

morgue (MORG) a place where dead bodies are kept before being buried

mortician (mor-TIH-shuhn) a person who prepares a body for a funeral

mummified (MUHM-*uh*-fahyd) dry and shriveled up

murky (MUR-kee) dark or cloudy

obscured (uhb-SKYOORD) covered up

reeled (REELD) moved unsteadily

renovate (REN-uh-*vayt*) to improve the condition of something

scalpels (SKAL-puhlz) sharp knives used to cut open bodies

stench (STENCH) a bad smell or odor

suffocating (SUHF-uh-kay-ting) being killed by having one's supply of air stopped

turret (TUR-it) a round tower on a building

vivid (VIV-id) bright and strong

ABOUT THE AUTHOR

Dee Phillips develops and writes nonfiction books for young readers and fiction books—including historical fiction—for middle graders and young adults. She loves to read and write stories that have a twist or an unexpected, thought-provoking ending. Dee lives near the ocean on the southwest coast of England. A keen hiker, her biggest ambition is to one day walk the entire coast of Great Britain.

ABOUT THE ILLUSTRATOR

Tom Connell has been a professional illustrator since 1987. He works in many styles, but his specialty is realism. Originally painting in gouache and acrylics, he moved on to airbrush and now draws most of his work digitally. He has created artworks for many advertising campaigns, magazines, and several hundred children's books. He lives with his family and two border collies close to the River Kennet in Reading, England.